Of Princes and Beauties

Of *Princes* & *Beauties*

Adult erotic faerie tales
edited by
Cecilia Tan

CIRCLET PRESS
CAMBRIDGE, MA

Of Princes and Beauties
Adult Erotic Faerie Tales

Circlet Press, Inc.
1770 Massachusetts Avenue, #278
Cambridge, MA 02140

Typeset and printed in the United States of America.

ISBN 1-885865-03-1

"The Frog Prince" (poem) by David Laurents originally appeared in
FirstHand, November 1994.

For more information about Circlet Press Erotic Science Fiction and Fantasy,
please send a self-addressed stamped envelope to the address above. Retail,
wholesale, and bulk discounts are available direct from us, or through
various book distributors including Alamo Square, AK Distributors,
Bookazine, Last Gasp of San Francisco, and many others.

Contents

The Frog Prince

~

DAVID LAURENTS

Lying naked atop the sheets in the summer heat
his lumpy genitals press against his crotch
like a frog crouched
in the thick reeds of his dark pubic hairs.

"Kiss me," they whisper,
"and I shall grow into a prince."

Stone Kiss

～

GARY BOWEN

*P*rince Alain sat in the crook of the battlements upon the highest tower of his father's castle, with only the gargoyles for company. A fitful breeze made his father's pennant flap in the wind: scarlet, with a rose and double chevron in gold. The same badge decorated the sleeve of Prince Alain's jacket: the uniform jacket of the Royal Hussars. The jacket was of deepest crimson, the color of spilled blood, fastened with real gold buttons in a tight row down the chest. His pelisse was thrown back over his shoulders, the golden lining gleaming in the sun. Fair hair fluttered in the wind, tangling in his small gold-and-ruby crown, streaming to his shoulders when still. He stared across the patchwork of fields and tidy little houses, each of them whitewashed, watching his doom draw nearer. The Princess Penelope was coming.

Her coach was accompanied by a troop of soldiers in sky-blue-and-silver uniforms, with the primrose yellow linings of their pelisses flapping as they posted along the road at modest speed. A thin skirmish line of flankers loped through the fields on either side of the road, leaping ditches and fences and scattering the common folk trying to earn a living. But the petty kingdoms of the region were at war, and King Joshua was taking no chance that rivals might disrupt the alliance between Mervyn and Corwyn by assassinating the intended bride.

"I don't want to marry a princess," Prince Alain told the stones. "In fact, I don't want to marry anybody at all. I'll go to fight, if that's what Father wants; he doesn't have to auction me off to the Princess of Corwyn."

But nobody answered, and the white coach with its silver trim glinting in the sunlight drew ever nearer. At last it trundled up the cobblestones of the High Street, rolling up the hill to the castle itself. The great drawbridge was down, and the Royal Guard was formed up to meet her. The King and Queen of Mervyn descended the steps from the great hall to meet her. But Alain remained where he was.

King Henry handed down the Princess himself. "My dear girl, we are delighted to have you. But where is your father?"

"Fighting the Hanns at the River Knauklin," she replied grimly. "My lord, he begs you dispatch your troops with all speed, and urges you not to stand on too much ceremony with regards to the marriage, else the dower lands will fall to the Hanns before you can claim them."

King Joshua stroked his yellow beard. "Grim news, Princess Penelope, grim news. Very well. We'll march at dawn."

Princess Penelope looked around, the pearls in her headdress gleaming over red hair restrained by a decorative net. "And which one is Prince Alain?"

"He, ah, has not finished his toilette," Queen Marguerite replied. "He will join us shortly."

The King snorted. "More likely communing with the gargoyles again," he humphed.

"Gargoyles?"

King Henry humphed again. "He has a poetical turn of mind. But don't worry, I've assigned Lord Constance as his military advisor."

Princess Penelope shielded her eyes with one slim hand, the long pointed sleeve anchored by a silver ring around her middle finger. She scanned the many towers and turrets, noting the fantastical beasts carved upon the walls, and said, "Yes, they are poetical. Where might Alain be?"

"The tallest one. He knows I won't climb that many steps coming after him."

"Then I shall. Show me the way."

Prince Alain was leaning on his elbows, looking over the top of the battlement at the face of a particularly hideous creature. Deep crevices marred its features, and its nose had broken off some time ago. Huge ears flared from the head, and tusks protruded from the lips. Slanted eyes took up an inordinate amount of space in the sloping skull, reminding Prince Alain a bit of a dog, in spite of the elephant ears. The body was equally powerful, long sinuous, dragonlike limbs, a spiked tail, and the sexual organs of a man, with a small row of barbs around the tip of the penis. It was poised as if climbing up the side of the tower, pausing to look back over its shoulder and snarl defiance at the humans below. Sighting between its ears, Prince Alain had a perfect view of the white carriage, and the pale princess who descended from it. Then his father, mother, and bride all went in together, and he knew he ought to go down before his father sent an "honor guard" to fetch him.

"I wish I were a gargoyle," he muttered. "I'd never come down."

The Princess Penelope paused to rest on the landing, looking up at the light spilling down from the roof. One more flight of steep stairs and she would be there. Of course, the Prince might not be, and her resolve hardened. She'd find King Henry's prissy boy if she had to climb every tower in the place. Poetical fancies were not going to come between her duty as a princess and the salvation of her kingdom. It didn't matter if Prince Alain were a fit ruler or not; all she needed was his army and his son and he could have his books and fancies. Taking a deep breath she settled her headdress more firmly on her head, straightened the falls of the dress so that the white-and-pale-blue satin hung in graceful drapes, and, holding her head high, mounted the steps, and, lifting her skirt enough to show her white stockings and dainty shoes, ascended to the roof.

She was greeted with the sight of a pair of scarlet breeches pulled tight over shapely young buttocks, the toes of black boots digging into the space between stone blocks, while the upper body disappeared from view.

"What are you doing?" she asked in surprise.

Prince Alain startled, nearly losing his grip. Vertigo seized him, and he closed his eyes tightly, fearing that he was about to plummet to his death. "Well, at least I won't have to get married," he told himself in consolation. Then his nerve steadied and he hauled himself back in, and dropped to the floor. "You startled me."

"Are you Prince Alain?"

"Yes, I am," he answered self-consciously, straightening his jacket and raking his fingers through his hair. He picked up his crown from where he'd left it sitting in the embrasure and put it on his head. "Yes, I'm Prince Alain," he answered with more dignity. "Who are you?"

"I'm Princess Penelope."

"Oh."

She crossed the space and looked over the wall where he had been hanging, flinched at the sight of the gargoyle, and said, "Charming creature. Is this the companion who makes you late for your own wedding?"

"It's supposed to be good luck if you can actually kiss the creature," he mumbled in embarrassment. "It's easy to kiss the top of the head, and when we were boys we often did, but nothing ever happened. So I thought maybe you have to kiss it on the mouth. You know, a real kiss." He blushed.

"Did it work this time?"

"I don't know, you interrupted me."

She craned her neck, trying to gauge to the distance. "You could fall and break your neck, you know."

"Yes, I know."

She looked him up and down, and was pleased to see he was as handsome as they had said. It would not be so hard to consummate her marriage and get on with the real business of ruling a kingdom. She held out her hand. "Shall we go down?"

He took her hand in his, holding it awkwardly. "All right."

They descended, hand in hand, Penelope determined to not let him escape until tomorrow.

The wedding took place in the great hall, the bishop presiding, with a limited number of guests, mostly ladies, in attendance, as the menfolk were busy preparing for war. To Prince Alain it seemed like yet another interminable court formality, and he went through it in a daze, speaking his lines as ordered. It was not until they were alone in the bridal chamber that the enormity of the deed began to sink in: he was alone in his bedchamber with a woman, and she was taking off her clothes.

He gulped, and sprawled in a generous armchair. "Will you not disrobe, my lord?" Penelope asked him, letting the bright gown fall, revealing a gauzy chemise. The light of the candles behind her shown through the fabric, silhouetting her woman's body.

"In a minute," he replied. He unbuttoned, for suddenly his collar seemed to be strangling him.

She crossed to him, and finished unbuttoning his jacket for him. Then she straddled his legs and sat upon his lap. She reached up and pulled the pins that held her headdress in place, and red tresses came cascading down. "Am I not beautiful?" she asked.

He nodded.

She set the precious ornament on the table at his elbow, then untied the string around her neck. The chemise slid down her arms, catching a moment on her nipples, then fell loose around her waist. Prince Alain found himself eye to aureole with a pair of pink nipples supported by soft breasts. "I've never kissed a woman," he said hoarsely. "I'm not entirely sure what I'm supposed to do."

"Didn't your father speak to you?"

"He said it was just like what the dogs and horses do, and I shouldn't worry about it, instinct would carry me through."

The Princess Penelope made a moue of displeasure. "I am not a bitch nor a mare. I require a more intelligent kind of lovemaking." She picked up his hand and cupped it around her breast. "Does that feel nice to you?"

"Yes, it's very soft." Slowly he lifted the other hand and cupped the other breast. She leaned into his hands.

"Now kiss them."

He dropped soft, dry kisses upon each of them.

"Again. Slower, longer, wetter."

He pressed his face against her flesh, pressing as she directed, feeling something warm and pleasant stir inside him. Experimentally he kissed her again, brushing his lips and cheek against her breast.

"That's it. Enjoy yourself."

He rubbed his face against her soft flesh, thinking to himself that he'd never seen a dog or horse do anything like that, and that his father's advice was proving inadequate, as he had feared. Gradually he discovered that wet kisses and a soft sucking had a pronounced effect upon the Princess, and curious about the process, experimented with different touches and tastes, until he noticed a damp spot seeping through her chemise and onto his legs. "That's it," she whispered. "Are you ready?"

He wasn't. But the Princess Penelope was equipped with a mother's advice, and sliding from his lap, she knelt before him and opened his breeches. He blushed bright pink, but cooperated as she exposed his legs, dragging his trousers down to the top of his boots. He jumped in panic when she leaned forward and took his organ into her mouth. He gripped the arms of the chair tightly, and thought about calling for help, then sat very still as heat percolated through his body and the purpose of her odd behavior manifested itself in a growing erection. He avoided looking at her, but closed his eyes and felt the extension of his body he had hitherto only experienced in particularly vivid dreams.

The Princess stepped out of her chemise and, standing before him clad in nothing but her white stockings and blue garters, her red hair falling about her shoulders, cupped her breasts in her hands. "Do you want me now?" she asked.

Prince Alain, with his horn of manhood jutting up before him, felt only confusion, but he nodded obediently, knowing that was what she wanted him to answer. He did not move from the chair, and the Princess, seeing that it was all up to her, climbed back into his lap and sat down. The moist weight of her enveloping his cock disturbed him, and he closed his eyes again, fingers locked on the arms of the chair. He tried to draw to mind the images of animals mating, and found no resemblance between the actions of the Princess and the actions of the bitches and mares. She began to slide up and down on his shaft, her hands clutching the lapels of his shirt and jacket, her breathing coming harshly through her lips, and he watched her from under his lashes. There was a certain warm pleasure to the act, and he found her weight bouncing against his legs pleased him in a way he couldn't describe. It occurred to him that they were behaving the opposite of animals, for in this case the female had mounted the male.

He closed his eyes tight then, and tried to imagine himself as a bitch mounted by a bulldog, and found the image sent a fiery heat burning through his veins. Sweat broke out on his forehead, and his back arched, the crown slipping dangerously on his head. She humped him harder, and the dog image in his mind grew larger and grayer, and now it was a gargoyle that mounted him, pressing its barbed tip into his body. He cried out then, his hands clamping on her thighs as he struggled beneath her, lost somewhere between the dream of rape and the shuddering contractions of orgasm.

When he collapsed, Princess Penelope paused for breath. She hadn't completed her own pleasure, but it didn't matter. She carried his seed inside her, and with luck it would grow. He opened his eyes, and looked at her with a clear and penetrating gaze, a look that went right through her and beyond. "Are we done?" he asked quietly.

She nodded and climbed off of him. He stood up and pulled up his pants. "I have to get ready to march tomorrow." She twined a lock of hair between her fingers and nodded. She could not argue against such a plan. He left the room, tucking in his shirt as he went.

He wandered through the halls, passing servants carrying bales of supplies, and turned into his father's audience chamber. The King was in council, with twenty-odd lords clustered around the great table, and maps spread out before them.

"Ah, Alain. Good of you to join us. How is your wife?"

"Well, my lord."

The lords looked at his disheveled dress and snickered. His father eyed him fondly. "And the marital duties are satisfactorily accomplished?"

He seated himself at the opposite end of the table. "So she said."

The lords laughed and the King smiled. He took up his wine cup and said, "Let us toast the newly married couple, and wish them children as rapidly as God sees fit."

16

"Hear, hear!" the lords cried, and drank the toast.

They laid out the battle plan for him, which was simple enough: march down the road to Corwyn until they found the fighting, and attack. Prince Alain would remain behind to receive and train the levies, which would need to be drilled and equipped before marching into battle. The King would lead his Royal Hussars himself, marching immediately to reinforce King Joshua. "I trust you to bring the levies to me in good order when called upon to do so. Lord Constance will remain with you, and will assist you in whatever way you require. I suggest you follow the advice he has to give."

"Yes, Father." He was disappointed to discover war would not relieve him of the duties of the marital bed. "May I go now?"

The King smiled indulgently. "Certainly. A young husband ought to spend long nights with his wife. I am afraid your honeymoon will be cut short all too soon as it is. By all means, go."

Prince Alain rose from his seat and headed out the door, turning not left, toward the sleeping chambers, but right, toward the tower. Lord Constance followed after him.

Lord Constance was a sagacious young man, in the habit of keeping his mouth shut unless he had something useful to say. Concluding that this was one of those occasions whereby he might serve his king better with his silence than his speech, he followed Prince Alain to the tower, the preoccupied young Prince unaware of the silent footfalls behind him.

As for Alain, his brain was working at rapid speed, solving the complexity of the mad fantasy that had seized his brain. He went downstairs first, to the storeroom, and Lord Constance barely escaped detection by hiding in the shadows under the stair when the Prince returned with what he wanted: a coil of rope.

Slinging it over his shoulder, the Prince ran lightly up the steps, frequent practice making the trip a matter of little consequence to him. Lord Constance, equally fit, but not so accustomed to flights of stairs, found his thighs cramping before he reached the top, and limped slowly on, trying to massage his legs and climb the steps at the same time.

Prince Alain unslung the rope from his shoulder, and taking a moment to lean over the parapet, studied his goal: the twisted body of the gargoyle. He stroked the bald head with his hand, tracing the fierce lines of the face, locking his fingers against the hardness of the stone, and feeling the leap of pleasure in his body. He had no good explanation for the feelings he was feeling, but they were the strongest feelings he had ever felt, and so he continued, wrapping the rope about the parapet, tying it firmly, and then tying it about his waist. He leaned hard against the ropes and the knots held, so he climbed over the edge, pelisse fluttering about his shoulders, and clinging tightly to the rope, commenced the short descent to the gargoyle.

The night was dark, a small portion of the moon shining palely across the fields. He paused a moment, boots braced against the stone, feeling their firmness underneath, and liking it. There was a solid simplicity to the stone that appealed to him and answered questions inside him that had only been confused by the softness of women and the machinations of royalty. He understood then that life truly was as simple as the mating of dogs, and the complexities of alliances and politics were needless complications to the art of war.

He stroked the gargoyle, ancient companion of his self-imposed exiles, finding in its form a twisted beauty he did not find among women. It gave him pleasure to caress its rough skin, to trace the bulges of muscles and to slip his fingers underneath the dark belly, groping between its legs for the spiked and hard length of its sex. Heat bloomed in his veins, and swelled in his groin.

He wrapped his arm around the gargoyle, feeling the thickness of its waist, the solidity of its stone flesh, and the coldness of its touch. He maneuvered his head underneath, into the shadows of its groin, and questing blindly, feeling his way with his lips, traced the erect phallus to its barbed tip. His tongue slid over the barbs, finding them blunt and harmless to his touch. He pressed his mouth over the end, engulfing it barbs and all, sliding it as deeply as he could. The stone had a bitter, dusty taste, but he persisted, feeling his own erection rise as he pressed the stone phallus into his mouth.

He settled his weight against the rope, felt it biting into his waist, and, with his mouth and one arm firmly clamped about the gargoyle, reached into his breeches and pulled out his own swollen flesh.

Of Princes and Beauties

Above him Lord Constance, keeping to the shadows, peered carefully over the edge, and when he ascertained what the Prince was doing, felt a bolt of revulsion pass over him, followed instantly by a stiffening of his interest and an inability to tear his eyes away. His breathing became labored and his clothes seemed tailored a size too small, and he longed to be rid of them. The image of the Prince's black boots braced against the wall, the flex of his muscles under the tight red clothes, the gleaming gold of his hair blazing against the dark stone bulk of the gargoyle burned itself into his mind. It astonished him that the amiable son of two perfectly proper people could indulge in such bizarre behavior, and show no sign of it in his features. He looked heavenward, but God did not reach down and smite him, and the Prince continued uninterrupted until his body throbbed and he splattered white streaks against the stone.

Prince Alain rested a bit, catching his breath and buttoning his breeches, feeling the relief of an urge that had long haunted him without him even being aware of it, except to know that the conventions of the court had left him stale and wanting. He leaned his head against the gargoyle, wondering what it meant that he was drawn to hard stone more than to soft flesh, but to that question he had no answer. He could only admit to himself that it was so. Surely his passion could not be unique, or the castle would not be decorated with such a profusion of monsters. He clambered back up the rope, his boot heels ringing on the stone, and saw Lord Constance.

The Prince straightened, tossing the pelisse back over his shoulders, and, picking up his crown, replaced it on his head. Constance's eyes were drawn to the unbuttoned space between the lapels of his jacket, where the paleness of his chest showed between the crimson halves of his jacket.

"You followed me."

Lord Constance nodded. "Your pardon, my prince. I did not mean to intrude."

Prince Alain crossed to him, and Lord Constance stood to attention. "You won't discuss this with my father. He wouldn't understand."

"No, my lord."

Prince Alain looked Lord Constance up and down. Several years the Prince's senior, he was hard bodied and experienced in war, with a small scar upon his jaw as proof of his courage. His dark hair was cut short to fit of his helmet, and the hour being late, a bit of dark stubble was manifesting along his jaw. His brown eyes were intelligent, his stance erect, and his brown jacket fit tightly over his chest, emphasizing broad shoulders and a narrow waist. His pelisse hung about his shoulders and tall, dark brown boots reached his thighs over buff-colored trousers. The line of his half-erect cock was pressed along his thigh, and the Prince studied it thoughtfully. "Do you like gargoyles?"

"Not as much as you do."

Prince Alain laughed. "Are you married?"

"No, my prince."

"Why not?"

"I never met the right girl."

"The right girl is the one who brings the best alliance to your house."

"So I have been told."

Prince Alain knelt before him, and pressing his lips against the leather of Lord Constance's trousers, kissed the bulging organ. The Prince traced it with his lips, and it swelled, growing harder and thicker, and the Prince found himself kissing it harder. His arm went around the young warrior's hips, and he found the body as firm and unyielding as that of the gargoyle. With his other hand he unbuttoned the leather, and pulled it to the tops of the boots. He fed the length of flesh to himself, sucking it intently, tasting the warm, salty taste of a living man, and finding it an improvement over the cold stone of the gargoyle.

Lord Constance's head fell back, and he breathed harder, thinking that that there was more than one way to cement an alliance, but he did not dare say so. Instead, when the young Prince rose and bent into the embrasure, he understood what was wanted of him, and mounted the Prince like an animal. Prince Alain gasped and cried out, and Lord Constance spit in his hand and lubricated the union of their bodies. Then he pushed hard, while Alain grimaced in pain and writhed beneath him. Constance found his self-discipline evaporating in the heat of the moment. He fucked hard and he didn't know if he was hurting the Prince or not, all he knew was that he has been asked for it, and he wanted to give it.

The pain melted into pleasure for Alain, and he braced himself on his elbows, liking the way his sex was smashed against the wall with each thrust, the minor brutality appealing to him far more than anything else during all his soft and pampered life. When at last Constance exploded and rested gasping against his back, he knew he would never be content to remain behind while his father went off to war.

"Get up," he said. Lord Constance rose and withdrew. "Your turn," he said.

"My prince?"

"You know what I want. Serve me as I served you."

Unfortunately, Constance reflected, an alliance with the royal house carried its price, as did all alliances. He knelt and sucked. He was hesitant about his task, and Prince Alain grabbed handfuls of his hair and held his head still while he thrust his cock back and forth between his lips. The Prince swelled easily, and thrust harder, Constance not resisting his assault. Alain savaged his mouth, and when he felt himself near to bursting, pulled the other man up and threw him into the embrasure. With one quick thrust he mounted him, Constance gasping in shock and clawing the stone. He had no experience in such matters, and the Prince's cock shoving into him was like being impaled upon a stake. He ground his teeth to keep from crying out, and prayed it wouldn't last long.

Prince Alain buried himself deeply in Constance's body, grinding his hips in a circle, then slamming deeper into the ravaged flesh. He hammered away at him, using his strength against him, then felt his sanity rip loose from its moorings, while the power roared through his veins. His orgasm went on and on, and left him spent, clinging to Lord Constance's broad back.

He rose and dressed, and Constance gratefully pulled himself together. He sat gingerly in the embrasure, not looking at his prince. He had always thought of the younger man as immature and silly; he had never guessed what depths of depravity lurked beneath the surface. Prince Alain settled his crown more firmly upon his head, and leaning against the wall behind Constance, placed a hand proprietarily on his shoulder. "I've learned things tonight of which I previously had no inkling. I don't like women. I don't like softness and I don't like politics. I'm going to war, and I'm going to be a king, and you're going to teach me how."

"Yes, my prince."

"Train me hard, because any mercy from you will only do me harm upon the battlefield. My father has been too lenient with me."

"You've the makings of a bold and bloody warrior, my prince."

He nodded. "I'd better be. Nothing less will defeat the Hanns. But I have another task first."

"My prince?"

"Come with me."

They descended to the Prince's bedchamber. He walked in without knocking and, taking a taper from the fireplace, lit a candle. "Penelope, wake up."

She stirred, and lifted her head. "Alain?"

"It is. And this is Lord Constance."

She sat up in bed, holding the covers over her nakedness. "My lord?"

"I need an heir, and I'm going off to war soon."

"Yes," she agreed cautiously.

"Lord Constance will help."

She eyed him dubiously. "What exactly did you have in mind?" Constance also gave the Prince a questioning look.

"He will come to you every morning, and do a husband's duty by you."

"What?" she exclaimed.

Lord Constance closed his eyes and wished he could melt through the floor. "But, my prince, she is your wife."

"And I don't like her. That's going to make it difficult for me to beget an heir, isn't it?"

"If I have offended you—" she started.

"Since I'm going to save your country, you ought not object too strenuously."

She shut her mouth.

"My prince, you put me in a difficult spot," Lord Constance protested.

"You're a virile man, are you not?"

"Yes, but—"

"Then what's the problem? She wants me to save her kingdom. I need an heir. You're supposed to help."

"I see your point."

Prince Alain wrapped his arms around Lord Constance. "It will work, you'll see."

Penelope's eyes narrowed. "Fine. Go back to your gargoyles, you twisted thing." She rose naked from the bed and held out her hand. "I want a man in my bed, not a monster."

Alain released Constance, and the warrior lord reluctantly stepped forward, drawn by the hand of the Princess. He gave one last helpless look over his shoulder, then tumbled into bed with her. She sprang upon him savagely, and his cock immediately answered her attack. Seeing that things were going satisfactorily, Prince Alain returned to the tower, and spent the rest of the night staring at the stars, keeping vigil with his stony companions.

Someday
My Prince
Will Come

~

EVAN HOLLANDER

O nce upon a time, there lived a well-hung and vibrant young man named Prince Eros.

Prince Eros had almost everything a young man could desire—good friends and wealth, his health, and dozens of beautiful and willing ladies to fuck.

But, alas, young Eros had one rather serious problem.

One night, after sneaking through the dimly lit castle halls to the chambers of Clitora, his sister's busty lady-in-waiting, Eros was made aware of his problem for the very first time.

As he pumped his long, thick cock furiously in the deep valley between Clitora's generous mounds of breastflesh, he found that as much as he wanted to, he could not come. He had been fucking the lady-in-waiting for several hours and although she had orgasmed three times, he had not joined her in that most delicious of carnal experiences.

Now, as the warm glow of the first morning sun peaked over the Kingdom's eastern horizon, Eros had become weary and wanted nothing more than to shoot his white-hot love liquid across Clitora's massive bosom and watch her rub it onto her great dark areola and nipples.

The thought edged him closer, but never over the fine line into climax.

Even as Clitora halted the tit-fuck and took Eros's princely cock in her hands and licked it with long, wet strokes of her tongue, he could not come. Even as she sucked on his cockhead and then took his entire length into her moist, warm mouth, he could not come.

Clitora didn't seem to mind the fact that Prince Eros's cock was still as hard as diamond and she seemed content to continue sucking on it long into the daylight hours. But the young Prince had a prior engagement with Madam Vulva at her country manor later that morning.

"I must go now," Prince Eros said finally as the sun rose fully over the horizon.

Clitora emptied her mouth of cock only long enough to speak. "But you'll be leaving unsatisfied," she said. "I can't possibly allow you to leave my chambers like this. What of my reputation? If others found out, I'd never have another caller."

Eros got up from the bed and began dressing. "On my word of honor, what has happened here—or perhaps I should say what has not happened here—will go with me to my grave."

◌

The ride to Madam Vulva's manor was a bumpy one and the small coach bounced and rocked on the road. By the trip's midway point, Prince Eros's cock had returned to its normal size, but his thoughts were still firmly fixed on his encounter with Clitora. Not being able to come just wasn't like him, he was used to having four to six orgasms per night. Once, he'd come eight times with five different women, an unofficial yet highly sought-after record among male members of the royal family.

While the ability to stay rock-hard through the night at first appeared to be a blessing, there came a point where one wanted the overpowering sexual tension to be released. Furthermore, Prince Eros was of marrying age and his father had been pressuring him of late to find himself a bride. What good would a bride be to him if he wasn't physically capable of fathering children to maintain the royal bloodline? Prince Eros had no answer. All he could do was hope that his problem would correct itself—and quickly.

As the coach neared Madam Vulva's manor, the Prince's heart—and loins—began to fill with new hope. Madam Vulva was an older woman and the most experienced sexual partner the Prince had ever had. Madam Vulva had also been the one to take the Prince's virginity (the incident occurring in the back of the coach on a particularly long trip to the King's summer residence by the sea) and would surely know just the remedy for what ailed him.

Of Princes and Beauties

The coach pulled up the drive and stopped in front of the front door of the manor. Madam Vulva's chambermaid was there to meet it.

"Madam is waiting for you in the salon," said the chambermaid.

The Prince looked the woman over closely. He'd never noticed her before. She was quite beautiful. Her eyes were large pools of sky blue and her hair was a deep shade of red that suggested a healthy, lusty fire burned deep within her bosom. The Prince couldn't decide whether she was petite or husky, but something about the way she carried herself suggested she was slightly better-endowed than most of the women in the land.

"And what might your name be?" asked the Prince, feeling his cock beginning to swell at the sight of the woman's warm, friendly smile.

"Sensua," she answered, bowing slightly.

"What a lovely name," the Prince said, his gaze fixed on the generous amount of decolletage.

"Thank you," she said, returning the Prince's smile. She led him to Madam Vulva's salon.

"Goodbye, Sensua," the Prince said as the chambermaid left him.

The woman must have noticed the swollen knot of cock between the Prince's legs—the skin-tight leotards not being the best article of clothing for purposes of humility—for she suddenly blushed and put a hand over her mouth. "Goodbye, Your Hardness, Uh ... I mean Your Highness," she said, turning and quickly running down the hall.

The Prince took a deep breath and opened the door to the salon.

Madam Vulva was lying on the bed wearing black stockings and a bone-white corset that pushed her two mountainous breasts together until they looked to be at the bursting point. Her legs were spread enticingly and her genitalia—proportionally as large as her two huge tits— looked as if it were aching to be fucked. She smiled coyly at the Prince and passed a hand gently over the tops of her breasts and then traced her index finger down the deep valley between them.

"Come over here," she said. "Show me what it's like to be young and virile, and I'll show you what it's like to be mature and wanton."

The Prince nearly ripped his clothes free from his body. Seconds later he was lying next to the woman, sucking on her thumbtip-sized nipples and fingering her sopping wet cunt with four of his fingers.

"How long has it been?" she moaned, tracing a line with her tongue along the Prince's neck and chest.

"Too long," the Prince replied, kneeling on the bed and guiding his throbbing dick into the wanting wet lips of her sex.

He arched his back as the lady took him deep inside her, the muscles of her vagina squeezing his cock and pulling it even deeper. The Prince could feel an orgasm starting to gather strength somewhere down near the soles of his feet. A broad smile broke across his face. Relief at last, he thought, as he placed his palms flat on Madam Vulva's breasts, squeezing them softly as he pumped the entire length of his cock in and out of her cunt.

Hours later, the Prince still had not come. He continued to pump, hard and deep, into Madam Vulva's bucking lovehole, sending her into the throes of yet another wild orgasm, but he was still no closer to coming than when they had first begun.

After Madam Vulva came for the fifth time, she begged the Prince to stop.

"Please, for the love of god...," she said, panting a hard staccato rhythm, her body slick and glistening with sweat. "I'm almost forty years old, have mercy on me."

The Prince complied with Madam Vulva's wishes and stopped.

"It's an odd problem to have," Madam Vulva said later, rubbing a soapy hand across her shoulders and breasts as they bathed together in the large claw-footed tub in the corner of the salon. "I've heard of men not being able to get hard and I've known plenty of men who came too quickly, but I've never heard of a man not being able to come at all. I didn't mind it so much, but I can't imagine what you're going through."

"I suppose I'll have to tell Father. He has expressed a wish that I be married soon," the Prince said with a sigh.

"Well, if you must tell him, I suppose the sooner you do it the better."

"Yes," said the Prince, rising from the tub. "You're right. I must tell him at once."

∞

When Prince Eros told his father of his problem, the King was at a loss over what to do.

"You could not come? Even with Madam Vulva?" the King asked as he stroked his long salt-and-pepper beard.

"Yes, Father. Even with Madam Vulva."

The King took a deep breath and sighed pensively. If Madam Vulva had been unsuccessful, the matter was a grave one indeed.

The King paced the floor of his son's chambers for several minutes, obviously deep in thought. His hand moved from his beard to the back of his neck and once again to his beard as he tried desperately to think of a solution.

"I could see the Wizard, perhaps he has a cure—"

"None of that," the King said quickly. "I can hardly imagine what price you'd have to pay for a spell that remedied a problem of that nature." He paced the floor for several more minutes.

Suddenly, the King froze in the middle of the room and clapped his hands together. They made a sound like thunder.

"Consul!" he shouted.

A door at the far end of the room creaked open and an old gray-haired man, bent over slightly at the waist, shuffled in.

"Yes, Your Majesty."

"I will only say this once," the King said. "So listen closely."

Consul nodded.

"My son is having trouble achieving orgasm." The King stopped to measure Consul's response.

Consul simply nodded, awaiting the King's next word.

"So I make a proclamation to all the ladies in the Kingdom. The first young woman who can make my son achieve orgasm will be his bride ... and future queen."

"But, Father—"

"Hush," the King said, placing a hand out in front of him to signify the matter was not open for discussion.

The Prince slumped back in the chair he was sitting in. "Very well."

The King turned to Consul. "Are you clear on what you are to do?"

Consul nodded, and shuffled out of the room.

In weeks the King's proclamation had reached the far corners of the Kingdom and scores of young ladies made the trek to the castle to try their luck. There were lithe blonde maidens, dark black-haired beauties, busty young redheads, and all manner in between.

The Prince "interviewed" fourteen hopefuls in the first week, twelve in the second. He was now midway through the third week and he was no closer to coming than he'd been at the start of it all.

"Bring in the next," the Prince said, taking a sip of water and lying back down on the bed.

The door opened and a woman more beautiful than any he'd seen before walked into the room. She had waist-length blonde hair that shimmered and shone as it cascaded over her shoulders and flowed down her back. She had piercing slate-gray eyes and skin as light and fair as hand-polished marble. She was dressed in a thin gown of green silk that clung tightly to her body and clearly showed her thick erect nipples as they pressed against the fabric.

"I am the Contessa Felatia," she said in a soft, breathy voice.

The Prince's cock was as hard and as stiff as his broadsword. He pulled aside the covers to reveal his phallus to the beautiful young Contessa.

In seconds the Contessa's gown was crumpled into a heap on the floor and she was crawling across the bed toward him.

The Prince's cock stood erect between his legs like a pike of the honor guard.

The Contessa wasted little time in taking the Prince's cock and running her velvety soft lips up and down the length of it. Soon, it was slick with moisture. Then she clasped the base of it with both hands and took the swollen purple head in her mouth and began pumping up and down on it like the piston of a water-powered grist mill.

The Prince arched his head back and tried to pump his cock into her mouth but he couldn't keep pace with her frenzied sucking. Instead, he leaned back and waited for himself to reach orgasm.

He waited...

And waited...

But he did not come.

Of Princes and Beauties

He had been sore for some time when he finally had to tell the Contessa Felatia that she had been just as unsuccessful as the others.

With obvious disappointment, she pulled her mouth from his cock with a loud slurp, slowly picked up her clothes, and saw herself out of the room.

The Prince tried to get some rest, but he tossed and turned through the night, never quite falling asleep.

In the morning he was awakened by a knock on the door.

"Come in," the Prince said sleepily.

Consul shuffled into the room. "A woman to see you. She's not a lady, but she says she knows you."

"Tell her to come back later with the rest of the women," the Prince said, rolling onto his stomach.

"That's just it, sir—there are no more ladies. She is the last one. The only reason I considered her was because you still have your ... problem."

The Prince sighed. "Very well, let her in."

Consul nodded and turned to leave.

"Do you know her name?"

Consul turned back around again. "She said it was Sensua, sir."

The Prince vaguely recalled the name, but from where he couldn't be sure.

Just then the door creaked open and the woman, Madam Vulva's chambermaid, entered.

The Prince immediately remembered the woman and the memory of her beauty on the morning of his last visit to Madam Vulva's manor quickly had him hard.

She stepped into the center of the room wearing a long black cloak clasped around her neck. The Prince was about to tell her he did indeed remember her when she undid the clasp and allowed the cloak to fall to the floor.

The Prince gasped.

She was dressed in black, wearing shiny black shoes with fashionably high heels. Her stockings were black, held up by lacy black garters. Her underpants were a wispy triangle of sheer black material that only faintly hid her mound of curly black hair and the folds of soft pink flesh beneath. Higher up, her black corset opened widely down the front, showing off her two huge tits to perfection and allowing just a hint of areola to peak out from beneath the thin black fabric.

Without saying a word, the woman pulled aside the fabric of her corset to allow her big breasts to stand free, firm and round on her chest. With the middle finger of her right hand she traced a slow circle over her left nipple until it condensed into a long, hard nub.

The Prince felt his pulse quicken.

Then she took the middle finger of her left hand and repeated the circular movement over her right nipple until they both stood erect like two brown thimbles. That done, she began rubbing her nipples between her thumb and forefingers, squeezing and pulling on them until they pointed at the Prince like a pair of arrow tips.

The Prince unconsciously placed his left hand over the knob of his shaft.

The woman Sensua continued working her breasts, rushing her open hands over the entire area of her globes, making it look as if the massage was making them bigger still.

The Prince's hand began moving up and down his shaft.

The woman stepped closer to the bed, lifting her right leg and letting her knee come to rest on the edge.

With her left hand she traced a line between her breasts down past her belly and on to her dampened sex. With a gentle movement of her hand she pulled aside the material covering her cunt and began to finger her clit, first with the tip of her middle finger and then running the entire length of the finger against it.

With her right hand she hefted her bulbous right breast until the swollen nipple was inches from her ruby-red lips.

The Prince's fist pounded up and down on his rod, faster and faster.

At first she merely flicked the tip of the nipple with her tongue, leaving a glistening spot of saliva on the end of it. Then, as her breath began to quicken and her hand moved harder against her clit, she took the entire nipple in her mouth and sucked on it.

The Prince continued to move his hand over his cock. An orgasm was building somewhere deep within him.

She lifted her left hand from her sopping wet cunt and grabbed her left breast forcefully, squeezing it like a pillow. She did the same with her other hand, turning her head to the side and beginning to moan and gasp as if she herself were about to come.

The Prince felt his legs beginning to tremble.

A few moments later, she let go of her tits, leaving them to heave up and down on her chest with each gasping breath, and moved both her hands down between her legs.

"Oh," she moaned, middle fingers pulling apart the lips of her sex and pressing her index fingers down hard on her clit.

"Oh," she moaned again, almost a scream this time, bringing her arms together and squeezing her tits between them like a pair of water-filled sacks.

The sight was just too much for the Prince to bear.

He grabbed the base of his throbbing, pulsing cock with both hands, arched his back, and let go.

The stream of jism was thick and long and hit the woman Sensua squarely in the chest. Nearly knocked back by the force of the blast, she quickly recovered and began to rub the sticky white liquid onto her sweaty breasts as if it were a salve.

The sight of her rubbing cum—his cum—onto her tits made the Prince come even longer and harder. He shot bolt after bolt through the air, weeks worth of cum coming out of him like a mighty river that had broken through a dam.

When it was over, the Prince fell over on the bed in a heap. He was spent.

When he awoke sometime later, the woman Sensua was lying next to him draped in a robe.

He opened his eyes and looked up at her, smiling. "How did you know what to do?" he asked, giving the nipples of her bloated breasts a lick.

She cradled his head in her hand so he could continue sucking on the nipple.

"Your problem wasn't down there," she said, taking his limp dick gently in her hand. "Everyone thinks this is a man's biggest sexual organ, but it's not. It's this." She pointed to his head. "I knew what you wanted the first time I saw you look at me."

"I'm forever in your debt," the Prince said. "Allow me to repay you in part by taking your hand in marriage."

"I accept," she said eagerly. Then a look of puzzlement crossed her face. "But if that's payment in part, how else will you repay me?"

"Well, you made me come. The least I can do is return the favor."

The Prince rolled over on the bed, took his rapidly growing cock in his hand, and guided it into the warm, soft folds of her cunt.

Needless to say, they came happily ever after.

The
Frog Prince
~

WANDA WOLFE

*P*rince Gerard was walking through the gardens when
he heard the sound of heartbreaking sobs. Being a
tenderhearted young man, he followed the sound to a small
well in the back corner of the rose garden. No one was there,
and he looked around in confusion before realizing that the
sobs were coming from a large frog which squatted on a
small bench next to the well. Gerard sat down on the other
end of the bench.

"Excuse me, Sir Frog, but you sound as if you're in great
pain. May I be of assistance?" he said.

The frog looked up at him and swallowed hard. "Not
unless you're a royal princess," he said.

Gerard smiled. "Well, I'm a royal prince. Does that
count?"

"Ah, you must be her brother then. You seem more courteous and kindhearted than she."

"You must be referring to my sister Esmerelda," Gerard sighed. "What did she do to you?"

The frog swallowed back more tears. "She dropped a golden ball in the well. I offered to get it for her if she'd repay me with a kiss, for only a kiss from a royal princess will remove this spell from me and return me to my rightful form as a man. She agreed, but when I fetched the ball, she grabbed it and ran away without kissing me, calling behind her that I was a fool to think any princess would kiss a horrid frog like me. I fear despair set in at that point, and I had to agree with her. I'm doomed to remain in this dreadful state for the rest of my life, unless I can find a way to end it all."

"Back up a minute," Gerard said. "How did you come to be a frog? And who were you before?"

The frog sighed. "I was Prince Reynold, from Cressina. I was considered a rather handsome man, I suppose, as you certainly are, Your Highness. One day a woman came to visit the palace who tried to entice me into her bed. She was far older than I, and I was accustomed to rebuffing such advances graciously, so I politely declined her invitation. But instead of accepting my answer, she grew furious and cast this spell on me. That I would turn into a frog and remain so until returned to my own form by the kiss of a royal princess."

"How did you come to be here?"

"There are no princesses in Cressina, so I set out to find one. This being the closest kingdom, I came here, and found my way into the gardens. It took me over a year to make my way here, only to be rejected by Her Highness." He broke into sobs again.

"There, there," Gerard said, his own eyes growing moist. "Don't despair. Perhaps we can think of a solution. I'll help you if I can. Can't let foul witches go around enchanting princes, after all."

Reynold swallowed back his tears again. "It's no use. No woman would ever kiss me, and certainly not a princess. The witch knew that. She just wanted me to be rejected, as I rejected her. Though the gods are my witness that I was gracious and courteous about it, and tried not to wound her feelings."

Gerard almost patted the frog on the head, then decided that would be patronizing to a fellow prince, even if he was a frog. "Well, let me talk to my sister. She's the only princess here, so it has to be her. I don't know if I can persuade her or not, but I'll do my best. She's a greedy little wench, in addition to being selfish. Perhaps if you offered her something in return."

"Whatever I have is hers in exchange. If she wishes, I'll take her home as my bride, and she'll be the Queen of Cressina."

Gerard shook his head. "She's already pledged to a prince in Tamron. Perhaps a diamond tiara, or some such. Will you give me leave to negotiate on your behalf?"

"Yes, of course. And you have my eternal gratitude, Highness. I'll do whatever you wish in return for your services."

Gerard shook his head. "I have no wish for anything. Doing a kindness is its own reward. Besides, I have three older brothers and am not likely to ever have the crown here. One of these days I may look elsewhere for a job, to get away from them. Knowing the future King of Cressina should increase my chances of a job there," he said cheerfully.

The frog hopped closer to him. "You have my word that you may have any job that you're qualified for, when I take the crown and have the right to offer such. My father is very old and won't live more than another ten years at most, so my time may come sooner than either of us expect."

"Why did he wait until he was so old to have a son?"

"He didn't. He had five others before me, but all of them are dead. And before you ask, I had no hand in any of their deaths. I was but five when the last one died. Two of them died in a plague there many years ago. One died in a hunting accident. One was killed by outlaws while on routine patrol. And the other died in a border skirmish."

Gerard smiled. "I believe you. Take heart now, and just stay out of sight. I'll come back tomorrow and let you know what progress I've made."

"Thank you, Highness."

"No need for titles between us. Call me Gerard."

The frog sighed deeply. "May the day come when we can ride together as friends, Gerard."

"I wish the same, Reynold. Rest now, and don't worry."

Gerard returned the next day and called softly to the frog.

Reynold hopped up out of the well eagerly, then settled into a dejected heap on the bench.

"I can tell by your face that the news isn't good," he said. "But I thank you for trying."

Gerard sighed. "I promised her everything but the moon, and she just closed her ears and refused to listen, saying she'd be the laughingstock of the kingdom if it were known. I swore we'd keep it secret and no one would ever know, but she just slammed the door in my face. I'm sorry, Reynold. Do you want me to go to Father and tell him the story? I don't think he'd appreciate her making a promise and then not keeping it. He'd make her kiss you."

"No, that would only humiliate her and make things worse. I can't do that. Thank you, Gerard, but I think it's best if I just find some big creature that likes to eat frogs, and end it all."

Gerard caressed the animal gently. "Don't even think that. Give me another day to think about it. Perhaps I can come up with a solution. If nothing else, I can carry you on my horse and we can go to Caledonia and ask one of the princesses there to do it. One of them might be a little more gracious. Though I have to admit every princess I've met has been as selfish and greedy as my sister."

"I know. The ones I've met have been the same. I despair of finding a decent wife, even if I ever do get out of this condition. I might marry a commoner, just to get away from them."

Gerard laughed. "I know how you feel. Listen, do you play chess?"

"I'm tenth rank, but I don't think I could move the pieces very well in this condition."

"I can move them for you. Come on up to my apartment and we'll play a few games. That ought to cheer you up."

They played several games, then Gerard arranged for supper to be brought to his apartment, and he shared it with the frog. Afterward, they talked late into the night, and the frog slept on Gerard's pillow.

The next day, Gerard tried again to get Esmerelda to keep her promise, telling her that the frog was in his apartment and no one would ever know. She made a face.

"I'd simply throw up if I had to kiss that horrid creature."

"That creature is Prince Reynold, the future King of Cressina."

"So he says. Personally, I don't believe a word of it."

"Did you ever hear a real frog talk?"

"No, and never got close enough to one to find out. And never intend to again. Leave me alone about it, Gerard."

The young prince sighed and went back to his room, shoulders slumped dejectedly. Reynold was weeping on the pillow. Gerard closed the door and stretched out on the bed, stroking the frog's head and back.

"Reynold, don't give up. We'll find a solution," he said gently. "I won't give up until we do."

"Gerard, you're the best friend I've ever had," the frog sobbed. "But nobody would ever want to kiss a creature that looks like this."

Gerard smiled and then his smile turned impish. "If she won't kiss you, I will," he said. "Even if it won't break the spell."

He leaned down and kissed the startled frog very gently on the top of the head.

A clap of thunder sounded in the room, startling both of them. And suddenly where the frog had been was the head of a handsome young man near Gerard's age. Huge blue eyes stared at Gerard in astonishment.

"Well, of all the—" Gerard began, and then stopped, laughing. "Who would ever have thought it? By all the gods, Reynold, you are handsome. And what a beautiful body."

For of course the prince was naked. Reynold looked down at himself, and his burgeoning cock, then looked back at Gerard.

"I suppose it's useless to try to tell you I don't find you attractive as well," he grinned. Then deep gratitude filled his face. "Gerard, how can I ever thank you?"

Gerard half closed his eyes. "Well, the other kiss wasn't very ideal. You could thank me with a real kiss," he murmured.

Reynold smiled. "I need a bath first. Then if you feel the same way I do, I'll thank you with more than a kiss."

Gerard returned the smile. "You're close enough to my size. Put on this robe, and we'll go down to the baths. I'll have the servants bring some food and wine up here, so it'll be waiting for us when we return."

Reynold sighed. "That sounds wonderful. It's been so long since I had a proper meal and some good wine. And even longer since I had an attractive ... friend ... to share it with."

Gerard grinned. "Esmerelda is going to be green with envy when she sees you."

Reynold laughed and threw an arm around his shoulders.

∾

In the bath, they soaped each other's bodies, hands lingering sensually on intimate places. Gerard let a soapy finger slip into the tight anus of the other, and Reynold moaned.

"Stop that or I'll come right here in the water," he murmured. "It's been over a year for me, remember."

Gerard laughed. "You're too pent up. Perhaps you should come, then later you can be more relaxed and we can make love properly."

He moved the finger faster, while his hand closed around the thick cock which swelled up from Reynold's enormous balls. Reynold lay back with a sigh, and accepted the ministrations. He came in less than a minute, spurting thick fluid out into the bathwater. He slumped down afterward, groaning with relief. Gerard laughed and rinsed the soap from both of them.

"Come on. Let's go back up to my room. We'll eat and then we can play to our heart's desire."

"I don't know. As long as I've been without, I can desire an awful lot," Reynold laughed. "But let's go have a try at it."

They went back upstairs to Gerard's room, where a small table had been set for two, with wine, cheese, fruit, and bread. Gerard poured wine for both of them, and then lifted his glass in a toast.

"To being a prince, instead of a frog," he said cheerfully.

"Thank the gods!" Reynold breathed. "And good friends," he added.

Gerard laughed and sipped the wine, then cut chunks of cheese for each of them.

"You are handsome," he murmured, as he nibbled the cheese.

Reynold looked at him from half-closed eyes. "No more so than you, my friend. You're not pledged to anyone?"

"No. I'm so far from the throne no one would want me. I'm pretty good with numbers, though, and like taking care of Father's accounts. I thought I might find someone who'd have need of a dependable and careful worker."

Reynold sat back and looked at him thoughtfully. "Yes. It would be good to have an overseer to take care of the books for me. Not only are there the books for the palace and the royal lands, but the books from the nobles have to be reviewed annually. I find it a nightmare myself. If I had someone I could trust to do that for me, freeing me to run the kingdom properly, I could be a far better king. Will you go home with me, Gerard?"

"When do you plan to go?"

"Father will be desperately worried about me. If you can lend me a horse, I need to start for home tomorrow. It's a two-month journey by horseback, and I've already been gone for a year."

"Better yet. Write to him and we'll send the letter ahead by swift courier. You can rest here for a few days and restore your strength, and then we can make a more leisurely trip of it. You're almost my size, but we'll have to have the seamstresses make a few modifications in a couple of things for you, until you get home to your own clothing."

"All right. I'll write to him tonight then, if you can arrange for a courier to leave in the morning."

"Yes. Let me go make arrangements for it while you eat, and then I'll hold you to that promise of a kiss."

He strode from the apartment and Reynold smiled, then began hungrily eating.

∾

Gerard returned just as Reynold was getting up from the table.

"Good. I timed it perfectly," Gerard laughed. "The arrangements are made. The courier will come here at dawn for your letter and then leave with two horses. By alternating horses, he can move much faster than we'd want to go. He should be there in six weeks, if all goes well."

He tossed aside his robe and caught Reynold close. "And now there was the matter of a kiss."

Reynold smiled. "Don't you want to eat? You barely nibbled a little cheese."

"I had a big lunch, and I'm not hungry. I ordered it for you. But what I am hungry for is the taste of you."

Reynold closed his eyes and leaned forward, his lips parted. Gerard groaned and covered Reynold's mouth with his, his tongue exploring hungrily. Reynold's arms slipped around him, one hand sliding down to caress Gerard's buttocks.

Gerard removed the robe from Reynold, then drew him onto the bed. "I've never wanted anyone the way I want you," he whispered.

His cock pressed against Reynold's belly, and Reynold laughed. "I couldn't tell," he teased. "You're so hard to arouse, I thought it would take me hours to get you in the mood."

Gerard laughed, and then slid down to tongue Reynold's hard little nipples. He bit them lightly, sucking them into his mouth, then nibbled his way down the taut abdomen to the hard cock and enormous balls. He sucked one of the balls, making Reynold groan with pleasure, then switched to the other and sucked it with equal abandon. He slid one finger into the tight anus, and then covered the thick cock with his mouth, sucking greedily. Reynold's breath was coming hard.

"Gerard, turn around so I can suck you, too," he panted. "I want to taste you."

Gerard swiveled around in the bed until his cock was near the other's mouth. Reynold closed on it ravenously, and Gerard's hips bucked in response. Reynold locked his arms around Gerard's body, holding him close, and plunged to the root, sucking with all his might.

Gerard exploded into his mouth, and when he felt the hot spurts of fluid, Reynold let go and let his own cock throb its way to release.

They held each other afterward, kissing tenderly, gazing into each other's eyes in blissful contentment. It was nearly half an hour later when Gerard felt the other's cock begin to stir. His own roused in response, and he grinned at Reynold.

"A lover with a passion to match my own. I never thought to meet one," he murmured. "Do you prefer to take or be taken?"

"I like both. Sometimes one, sometimes the other. And you?"

"The same. I think now I'd like to be taken, if you don't mind."

"All right. And later you can take me in turn. Do you like to get on your hands and knees, or lie on your side?"

"It depends on what I want. When I'm in the mood to be ridden like a prize stallion, I'd rather be on my hands and knees, so I can buck and thrash about. When I prefer something more peaceful and loving, I like to either lie on my side, or on my back like a wench. And sometimes, I like my partner to lie on his back, and let me impale myself on him. All are good, at different times. Since we've sated the initial passion, I think I'd prefer something a little more relaxed and loving. How would you like to take me?"

"On your back, I think, so I can stretch out and kiss you as I move in you. We'll move very slow and easy until it gets out of control, then hard and fast until we both come."

"Mmmm. I like that. I'm pretty tight. You'll need to use something. There's a jar of cream in the drawer of that table."

Reynold opened the jar and massaged some of the cream onto his cock, then rubbed it deeply into Gerard, who closed his eyes and sighed with pleasure. Reynold put the jar aside and settled down between Gerard's legs, easing the head of his cock into the tight anus. Gerard flinched, but opened to him, and even arched up a little to take more. Reynold smiled and pushed the rest of the way in. Gerard's eyes widened and his mouth dropped open in a silent scream of pleasure. He slumped back on the bed, his chest heaving.

"Be still for a moment, or I'll come," he panted. "Let me get control again."

Reynold dropped down on him and showered little kisses on his face. "Just tell me when you're ready," he whispered.

Gerard closed his eyes and gradually his breathing grew even again. He opened his eyes then and smiled up at Reynold.

"That never happened to me before. That I almost came just from being penetrated. Reynold, you excite me so."

"No more than you do me. May I move now?"

"Yes. I have it under control."

"Tell me if you lose it again, and I'll stop. I want this to last a long time."

He kissed Gerard deeply, then began a lazy movement, withdrawing no more than an inch before sliding back inside, his belly pressing against Gerard's cock as he moved.

"This is nice," Gerard sighed. "I could enjoy this for hours if we could keep it up."

Reynold chuckled. "You'd be sore if we went that long."

"It'd be worth it," Gerard smiled. "Kiss me again."

Reynold kissed him again, their tongues exploring each other's mouths.

They continued the lazy movement for nearly an hour, occasionally stopping for one or the other to regain control. Then Reynold smiled down at him. "I want to come now. All right?"

"Yes," Gerard whispered.

Reynold reached between them to stroke Gerard's cock, then began moving hard and fast. Gerard arched up to him, crying out in ecstasy as the orgasm overcame him. Reynold exploded into him, his balls feeling like they were draining completely as the orgasm went on and on. He collapsed down onto Gerard as it ended, his arms going around Gerard and his head resting on Gerard's shoulder. Gerard slipped his arms around Reynold, holding him close.

They fell asleep like that, and woke at twilight still wrapped in each other's arms. Reynold smiled down at Gerard.

"How could you sleep with me on top of you?"

"The weight was distributed enough that it wasn't a burden. Hungry?"

"For more of you first. Then food and drink."

"A bath and then food," Gerard corrected, laughing. "We can't go to supper smelling like we've spent the afternoon in pleasure, even if we have. Father might frown on it just a bit. I want to ride you, like my prize stallion."

Reynold smiled and moved off Gerard, coming up on his hands and knees. Gerard used the lubricant liberally, then slid into the tight anus. Once he was inside, he wrapped his arms around Reynold, gripping Reynold's cock, and started riding hard. Reynold gasped and bucked his hips madly, responding to the other's passion. Gerard pulled his cock almost out, then slammed it in, hard and fast. Reynold groaned and threw his head back, chest heaving with the force of his rapid breathing.

Gerard squeezed the cock in his hand, and slid his other hand down to massage the big balls under it. Reynold cried out, a wordless cry of passion.

Gerard started coming then, massive jets of fluid pumping out of him into the other's tight ass. Reynold whimpered as he felt it, and moments later, his cock started pulsating in time to it, thick fluid spurting out to cover Gerard's hand.

They slumped down on the bed afterward, panting, Gerard gently stroking Reynold's shoulder. When he could breathe normally again, Reynold smiled at him and ran long, graceful fingers through Gerard's hair.

"No one ever rode me so. I may never be the same," he said. "I'm glad you agreed to go home with me. No other lover could ever satisfy me after you."

Gerard smiled and kissed him. "Nor me, Reynold. Come, let's go have a bath and supper. Then you need to write to your father, and after that we can make love again."

"Yes. I want to lie on my back while you impale yourself on me, so I can play with your cock and balls while you ride my cock."

"Mmmm. That sounds good to me."

Of Princes and Beauties

They went down to the baths, then off to supper, where Esmerelda turned bright red with fury when she realized what a handsome prince she could have had if she'd been willing to kiss a frog.

Dictation

～

E R STEWART

The wizard had his dick out again.

When he does that, I usually lay low, because there's no telling what'll happen when it goes off. See, he doesn't so much ejaculate as explode. Oh, and the dick itself is, well, strange. It's not entirely of this world, for one thing. For another, it has a mind of its own. A brain, little eyes, everything. Apparently the wizard can see through those little eyes, which means he can fuck a wench from the village and actually see what she looks like inside.

Not that village girls volunteer for such scrutiny.

Shutting the door behind me, I sidled past the bookshelf and set the steaming cup of palewort tea on the nearest flat surface, the skull table. Glints of light glittered in some of those skulls, as if intelligence lingered where no brains or eyes remained.

"Sir, your tea," I said, in as neutral and disinterested a voice as possible.

Heaving back, his head lolling, the wizard grunted, but his dick twitched and glanced at me. I shuddered as it wiggled back and forth hard enough to flap the wizard's open robes. "Leave," the wizard grunted.

I left, one last glimpse showing the wizard's dick shrinking back from the size of a man to the size of a man's. From six feet to six inches in one easy splatter of ectoplasmic semen, which I'd have to clean up later, naturally. Where he splashed the walls it ate away at the stone, and it wasn't unusual to go through three or four new mops before getting the stuff up. And it crawled, too, but luckily it crawled slowly, sort of oozed like an amoeba.

What manner of protoplasmic life that semen of his might regenerate was something I didn't really want to know, but for sure the village girls he ravished would never know, because they usually went up in a burst of cold green flame about ten minutes after he schtupped them. It was a stylish way to go, but who wants to go in the first place?

I got a third of the way down the spiral stairs when the wizard bellowed for me again. Back up the tower staircase I climbed, panting.

He was out of breath, too, from having masturbated. "Clean that up, would you?" he asked, sipping the palewort tea and letting his beard and whiskers ripple like seaweed, which meant he liked the taste.

"Yes, sir," I said, slumping to the closet. When I yanked the wood door open, I saw only pitch blackness, a void so total that my head wanted to lean forward and fall into it. I squinted, looked sideways at the infinity closet, and stuck in my arm. A mop grabbed me, and I pulled it out. As soon as it was out of the infinity closet, it let me grab it, and became inanimate, a dead thing of this world.

Trying not to think about a world in which mops swam like squids, I started cleaning up the steamy mess the wizard's dick had made.

"Well," he said after a while, "how about we go wenching tonight."

If there had been any doubt of his otherworldly horniness, it vanished exactly as I shrugged and said, "Sure, boss. But maybe we ought to find another village. Elmbridge is getting kind of pissed off."

He grinned. His white beard, mustache, and fluffy eyebrows all rippled around his sunburned, wrinkled face. He raised gnarled hands and made a slight, slick gesture. "To the mirrors with them," he said. "The Elmbridge women are the sexiest."

I nodded and stowed the mop, feeling it jump from my grasp as I eased it into the closet. "They're the sexiest because of that spell of yours. Couldn't you cast that same spell on another place?"

He slammed down his teacup. Skulls rattled, and several of them floated upward, as if experiencing less gravity. "Did they put you up to this?"

"Who?"

"The Elmbridge elders?"

What could I say. Hell, yes, they'd asked me, begged me in fact, to try to get the wizard to pick on the young women of another village, at least for a while, but to admit it might cost me considerably more than my scrawny hide, considering his shifty moods, so I said, "I overheard their complaints when I went down the hill for supplies."

A sadness crossed his face. "Yes, I can see how they'd complain. The ghosts I send back aren't the same as flesh-and-blood daughters, I suppose. If ghosts sufficed, I'd fuck them instead. But what am I to do, Sauer?"

When he called me by my last name, Sauer, I knew he really wanted my opinion, so I said, "Why not go get your normal dick back?"

"Or die trying," he said, still not throwing a lightning-bolt fit, but actually considering my advice. "Would you come with me?"

As if I had any choice about it. "Of course," I said. My throat hasn't been that dry since the time he locked me in the desert room for spilling that last vial of dragon's blood.

I packed. Seven crates, each one stuffed with a different kind of herb, elixir, potion, or distillation. When I was done, I let him know, and the wizard came down (in a flash of black sparks, he who never uses stairs) and waved his hands over the crates. Each one glowed bright orange, and then faded away. "Travel light," he said.

I didn't know if he meant the glow or the weight, and didn't ask. All I knew was that the crates would now accompany us wherever we went.

It was quite a journey, too. The witch who switched dicks on the wizard lives on an obsidian mountain that jabs out of the Duendonian jungles. Normally the wizard just disappears one place and appears elsewhere, but because he needed all the magic stuff with him, we had to walk. Well, I walked. The wizard sat on a two-wheeled cart pulled by our little wyvern, which is nine feet long and looks like a flying snake, except that it kind of swims through the air.

My nerves were shot by the time we got to the foot of Mount Yagos, where the bad witch Aur lived, or dwelled, or manifested, or whatever that kind of being does when appearing to more mortal types.

Looking up, I shaded my eyes from the purple hot sun and said, "Sheer cliffs, smooth as glass."

"There are reflections, though," the wizard pointed out. It was true. The entire black mountain, shaped like a broken-off elephant's tusk, jagged side up, gleamed black and shiny, so it reflected the trackless jungles, the sky, the glare of sun, and even us.

Well, it reflected the wyvern and me, but the wizard appeared in the gloss in negative. You could see his bones. They weren't human. And you could see the crimson glint of his dick's eyes, hovering just inside his robes, tiny now but, with erection, big enough to throw him around as it thrashed in otherworldly ecstasy.

Muttering spells and fetching things from this or that crate, the wizard caused our reflections to stretch upward. Before I knew what happened, I was looking not at the mountain but at the jungle around it. My awareness had gone into the reflections, which were stretching upward, ever higher.

The view grew spectacular. I could see silver rivers, white falls, dark stones, brown boulders, and multi-green vegetation covering gently rolling land clear to the horizon. And then clouds obscured the view.

My perspective flipped again, and I was suddenly freezing cold. We stood on an escarpment high above the world, on Mount Yagos. Icy winds slashed at us. Snow and ice blew.

"Boss," I said, shivering. "We've got to find shelter."

"Nonsense," he said, not bothered by the temperature. He could sit in a campfire and bathe in Arctic waters; nothing fazed him when it came to this world's creature comforts.

He waved his arms around and yelled challenges to the witch. That went on for some time. Then a crack in the stone before us appeared, and we rushed in.

There was precious little heat coming from the single coal brazier hanging from the ceiling, but at least we were out of the wind. Our wyvern squealed the way they do and coiled in a corner for some temporary hibernation. I stood hugging myself, wishing I'd brought another cloak or three, and the wizard stalked around the big empty room.

We stood on an obsidian floor polished smooth as a mirror. Our reflections were distorted, and moved whether we did or not. The air was full of light from a source I could not locate. Rough walls surrounded us, and the ceiling was carved into grotesque faces, some human, most not.

"You know what I'm here to reclaim," the wizard said.

A woman's voice chuckled, low and throaty. "I can guess," the witch said, even as a form appeared before us, just suddenly there. Neither male nor female, the witch's skin was pea green, its hair was dark blue, and the nails on its seven-digit hands glinted bright yellow. Snaggled ocher teeth pushed lips aside. A forked tongue flicked. Vertical pupils split the eyes. "Darling," the witch said. "I knew you'd come back."

The wizard gave me a look that warned me to back off. I did, right into the arms of a naked woman twice my height, who whispered with a three-part voice, "And you're mine."

She turned me around and peeled my clothes off. It was both exhilarating and humiliating, but I could do nothing to resist her; she was not only twice my size, but muscular and quick and apparently used to manhandling. Once I was stripped, she rubbed me up and down on her as if I were nothing but an oversized dildo. Her pubic thatch rasped me up and scraped me down from chin to knees.

She set me on the floor. I gazed up at her. She was, believe it or not, kind of attractive, a regular face, full lips, narrow nose, green eyes. Her blonde hair was shoulder-length but bound in a single big braid. Her shoulders were more than twice as wide as mine, and they rippled with muscle. Her breasts, each one the size of my head, stood proud, if not arrogant. A single nipple filled my mouth, which I discovered when I moved forward and stretched up to suckle a bit, hoping to appease her. The last thing I needed was this woman feeling scorned.

"Uh," she said, closing her eyes in pleasure as I worked on her boobs, and her labia parted then, releasing musk that affected me like a jolt of sexual electricity. My boner popped up harder and bigger than it had ever been before, and suddenly I genuinely wanted this Amazon flat on the floor under me.

"Lay down," I told her, and she did, quick, so quick that I fell onto her and bounced a couple times.

My wiener was too small. Oh, it felt marvelous to me, in a way, but I thrust into her and she lay with an expectant look, as if waiting for the kidding to be over. I knew I had to do something, so I, well, I jumped in head first, so to speak.

Her clit almost gagged me. It was the size of my hand, and moved under my oral ministrations as if trying to escape me. Knowing this might not satisfy her, I gently eased my entire left arm into her slick vaginal depths, hoping that, when orgasm came, her contracting muscles wouldn't snap my bones like kindling.

While I was occupied with pleasing my Amazon captor, I heard strange grunts, shrieks, and sloshing sounds from the center of the floor, directly under the brazier of hot coals. Risking a glance, I was disappointed. I'd expected to see the wizard and the witch in each other's grasp, at each other's throats, tearing each other to bits for dominance, but instead all I saw was the wizard, standing stock-still, staring at me.

Well, it was embarrassing, but I looked away from his eerie gaze and got on with my job of pleasing the giantess.

My arm was sore already, so I switched, all the while licking, sucking, nibbling, and at times choking on her clitoris. As I pleasured her, I thought to myself, "This is how the wizard's dick must feel," and that's when I got kind of excited myself. The emotions carried me away. I pulled my arm free of her inner spasms. With a gulp of air, I pushed my face downward from her clit, until her labia split for me, until my face began entering her. I had no idea if my head would fit or not, but I wanted to try; right then it was the most exciting idea I'd ever had with a woman, and when would I ever get another chance to try it?

Kissing her deep, tasting nectar as intoxicating and thrilling as any potion or spell, I let my entire body make love with her, become her object of slippery, sexy joy.

My ears slipped in, and things got quiet. I forced my eyes open, but could see only a dim pink glow surrounding me. I heard her moans, filtered through the length of her. I felt her inner tensions around me, and I pushed all the harder, wanting only to fill her, fulfill her, please her beyond her wildest dreams.

I don't know when I lost control of the thrusting. First I realized, I was being pulled back. I felt no grasp on my ankles or anything, but without my consent and against my will, I was being pulled backward. It felt really good, though. Her squeezings caught me under the chin and on my cheeks, and as I was pulled through that grip tingles shot all through me, bringing my entire body closer to an overpowering orgasm.

And then, just as I started enjoying my forced with- drawal, I was shoved forward again. The tempo increased.

My eyes adjusted, and I could see the clenching tunnel in which I moved. I watched ripples of enjoyment flutter the sugarwalls around me, and the fact that I was the cause of such wonderful feelings made me want to gush, to pour myself forth, to spew my own secrets into her.

And that's just what happened, only it wasn't like vomiting, it was like coming harder and longer and better than ever before. I got light-headed and my senses swirled. I watched the stuff come from me, soaking her pink recesses, filling cavities sought but not quite found. And as I gushed, she orgasmed around me, clenching harder than I thought I could stand.

Breathing never entered my mind until I was pulled out of her. That's when I realized that I hadn't been breathing for some time.

Funny thing, though. I felt no urge to breathe. And that's when I realized something even weirder, even worse.

As I was pulled back from inside her pussy, I watched her fall away from me at an alarming rate. Perspectives shifted and depth perception stretched. She looked huge now, feet to my inches. The whole room seemed as big as a valley.

That's when I noticed the hand, the wizard's hand, slightly larger than I was, come down from above to grab and fold me. I was doubled over, and crammed back into a close, smelly place.

Yep, joke of jokes, I was back in the wizard's pants, where I'd originally come from. In more ways than one, I felt like such a dick for having fallen for such a trick. After all, in the original encounter, I, the wizard's dick, had failed to please the sexless, mirthless witch, so she had removed me. I got to stay with the wizard, but only as a servant. And in my place, the witch placed, what else, itself. That way, the witch could torture the wizard with horniness, and punish anyone who fucked him out of his frustration.

But now, because I'd pleased the Amazon aspect of the witch, the witch had switched us back, and while the wizard was now out a servant, he had gained a regular hose, one to which the girls of Elmbridge would not object. They could fuck the wizard a zillion times now, and not burst into cold green flame once.

"Thanks," the wizard said, snapping his fingers at the wyvern to rouse it for more pulling.

Aur the Witch raised a hand in farewell and said, "Come again soon," and then burst into gale-force laughter that stumbled, rolled, and otherwise pushed us, the wizard and me, out of the room. We descended Mount Yagos and returned to our castle above Elmbridge, and although I miss being able to run around loose, I must say there are compensations.

By the way, I'm writing this between orgasms. We've impregnated seven village girls tonight already, and I'm raring to ram a few more, but I thought I should chronicle my return to service.

And no, I'm not holding a pen in my tiny little vertical mouth: number seven's writing this. I'm just dictating.

Beauty
and the Beast

~

WANDA WOLFE

*I*t's funny how time tends to distort history. And how
we old men remember our youth with such clarity,
when we can't even remember what we had for supper last
night. Someday you boys will look back in fond memory
on these days, sitting in the garden listening to an old
man tell stories from his youth. But better the stories I tell
you than the nonsense that foolish bard spouts every night.
Like the one he told you about Beauty and the Beast last
night.

What? No, of course he doesn't know the real story. And
wouldn't care if he did. His version of it is a nicer one, more
acceptable to the common folk. They'd frown if he told the
truth, not that he ever would, of course.

Tell you the truth? You're both a bit young. How old are
you now, Tony? Eleven? Well, I suppose that's old enough

for you to hear such an adult story. In fact, we have to go back to when I was eleven to start the story.

Eleven is such a tumultuous age for a boy. The body is beginning to change, and feelings awaken for the first time, making you look at women and sometimes men in new ways, longing for something you aren't quite sure what. Your grandfather and I went through that, just as you boys are now. He was a month younger than I was, and perhaps it hit me a little sooner than it did him. But I began to notice him in a different way.

You see, I'd been placed in the cradle with him when he was born, destined to be his companion and servant. We grew up together, playing with the same toys, learning to love each other and fight with each other, just as you boys do. We learned the manly arts, and our tutor began the laborious job of teaching us such things as history and mathematics and geography and sorcery. Yes, the same things you boys are studying now.

Your grandfather—Ian was his name, though I called him always "Highness," as was proper—disliked our studies, preferring to practice with his sword or bow. But I took to the study of sorcery well enough, and learned many things. Some healing, a little skill with illusion, warding, and a few other such things.

Then we turned eleven, and suddenly I saw His Highness in a whole new light. I'd never before realized how beautiful he was. His hair was like yours, Tony, so black it looks blue in the sunlight. And his eyes were like yours as well, that deep warm brown flecked with gold. His body was beginning to take on some of the manly contours it would later have, and I found myself watching him at every available opportunity, with some strange longing in me that I didn't—or wouldn't—recognize.

If he felt the same thing, it was never toward me, of course. I was but his servant and companion. Always along when he went anywhere, always taken for granted as simply as he accepted his horse and his dog. I was just a part of him, as were they.

But he began experimenting then, with the noble sons who were here for training. They'd ride into the woods, with me along to guard them, and in some sheltered glen, they'd undress and teach each other about the joys of the flesh. And I'd ache inside, longing so to be a part of it. My young cock would harden against my belly and throb as I watched them. After a while I learned that if I stroked it as I watched, I could get release, with none the wiser.

We were thirteen when I had my first experience with sex. One of the warriors took me behind the stables. It was nothing like the carefree experimentation I'd seen between His Highness and his companions. Instead the warrior urged me to suck him, and he held my head, making me gag from it. When he saw my reaction to it, he turned me around and took me. And it hurt, very much. After he left, I sobbed for a long time before taking myself to the baths to clean up. And I made sure none of the warriors ever got me alone again, though some of them tried.

At night, it was my job to sleep across the doorway of His Highness's room. Sometimes he'd invite one of his

WANDA WOLFE ❧ *Beauty and the Beast*

friends to spend the night, or a wench, and I'd hear them playing in the bed. I cried sometimes, from the longing that filled me.

We were seventeen when the invasion came. A foul sorcerer and his army conquered the kingdom next to ours, and then moved on into ours. His Majesty called us to him, and charged me with taking care of His Highness. Then he sent us flying in the opposite direction, to hide until His Highness was old enough and skilled enough to return and retake the kingdom.

We fled for months, to a small kingdom far from home. There, with the money and jewels we'd brought with us, we bought a walled estate outside of a small city. And His Highness hired a sorcerer to continue our lessons in the craft, this time in earnest.

I didn't trust the sorcerer he hired. There was something about the man which rang untrue to me. However, it wasn't mine to judge, but to protect and to learn. I told His Highness of my distrust, and he merely shrugged it off. We studied with the sorcerer for a year, and I carefully hid from him how much I was learning, pretending that it was as difficult for me as for His Highness.

Then one day, he asked why we wished to learn sorcery, since we were obviously so unsuited for the craft. His Highness told him of the invasion of our kingdom, and that he had to learn sorcery before he could return and defeat the evil sorcerer who now controlled our kingdom. His Highness had no way of knowing what a terrible mistake it was to reveal himself to this sorcerer, who it turned out was a brother to the one who'd conquered our land. When he learned who His Highness was, he placed him under the foul spell, that by day he'd be a horrid beast, and only by night would he be a man. Having no fear of me, a poor servant, he left me there to guard the prince. He warded the walls of the estate so the prince couldn't leave it, knowing I wouldn't leave without him.

Oh, it was a most horrible day! His Highness went quite mad, I think. He rampaged through the gardens, killing and eating his own dog, destroying half the flowers. But when night came, he collapsed near the garden door, a man again, though exhausted and dirty and beaten.

I took him inside and bathed him as gently as I could, then put him to bed. He slept the sleep of the damned, too deep to suffer from nightmares. And just before dawn, he woke, and returned to the garden, where he again became the horrid beast.

The next few months were a living nightmare. I arranged for seven sheep to be delivered to us at the beginning of each week. We'd learned quickly that one sheep was what the beast needed for sustenance each day. I dismissed the servants, and took care of our needs myself. Whenever I had to go into town for supplies, I locked and warded the door carefully, both to keep him inside and to keep strangers out.

After a month or so, we'd settled into a routine of it, and I began to search for a way to save my master from the spell. It was a long and laborious process, since I had to tend to all our needs in addition to whatever I did in the way of study.

Nearly a year after he became the beast, I finally discovered a simple spell which would allow me to sleep but one hour and still have the benefits of a full night's rest. After that, it went a little faster, since I could tuck him into bed and then go straight to the study, working most of the night.

I was still working there one night when he appeared in the doorway.

"What are you doing?" he asked.

I bowed my head. "I suppose it's foolish of me, Highness," I admitted. "But I'm trying to find a spell which will free you from this curse."

His expression flickered through a number of emotions, and then he turned away and left me without comment. I took a deep breath, and continued what I'd been doing.

The rampaging of the beast during the day so totally exhausted his body that he'd been sleeping much of the night prior to this. But perhaps he was starting to get accustomed to it, for the next night he returned to the study again, shortly after midnight.

"Do you sleep during the day to make up for working all night?" he asked me.

I told him of the spell I'd discovered to allow me to sleep less. He looked at me for a long time, then nodded. "Teach it to me," he said.

I did, and after that, though he still needed more sleep than I did, he worked with me at night, trying to find the answer.

During this time, when I bathed him at night, I couldn't help noticing that he was suffering more and more from the lack of any sexual outlet. At last, one night, as I bathed him, I washed his cock carefully, then left my hand around it, moving it gently. When his only reaction was to close his eyes, I moved with more assurance, soon giving him the release he needed. Afterward, I simply continued bathing him as though nothing had happened. He said nothing of it, and neither did I.

Each night after that, if his cock was hard, which it usually was, I did the same for him. And neither of us mentioned it.

When he'd been the beast for two years, the strain told on him. He went quite mad again, and tore through the garden all day long like a crazed animal. When dark came, he collapsed at the garden door, his body shaking and trembling. I had to carry him to the bath. I washed him tenderly, then helped him out and dried him off. He leaned on me as I helped him to the bed. When he collapsed face down, I got some scented oil, and began giving him a massage.

He sighed with appreciation. He'd always loved massages. I'd never given him one before, but I'd seen the bath wenches do it, and just did what they'd done. When I finished with his back and legs, I asked him to turn over. He did. His cock was standing up hard and red, and I had to stifle a moan when I saw it.

I massaged the front of him with the same thoroughness, then moved back to his cock at last. I massaged his beautiful balls gently, loving the feel of them in their giant sack. Then I tenderly touched his cock.

He moaned. It was the first time he'd made a sound when I gave him release. I stroked the cock with my hand slowly, and then hesitantly lowered my mouth to suck the head. His pelvis arched up to me, and I took more of it, losing all control of myself. It was his cock in my mouth, my beloved master's, the one I'd wanted to suck for all those long years. I sucked greedily, and all too soon the hot fluid spurted from him, filling my mouth and throat. I swallowed hungrily, loving the taste of him. And very slowly, I released him and then drew a sheet up over him.

His eyes were closed. I stared down at him for a long moment, knowing from the even movement of his chest that he'd dropped into sleep the instant the release had come. Tears fell from my eyes then.

I leaned over and kissed his forehead lovingly, then slipped from the room to go to the study.

It was well after midnight when he joined me, more relaxed than he'd been in a while. Common sense told me it was the beast's rampage which had purged him of the wildness which had been steadily building up in him. And yet a part of me persisted in thinking that it was my love which had given him a little of that peace.

The bard tells that the merchant came into our garden and stole a rose. I've already told you that such was impossible, since the entire estate was sorcerously warded from intrusion. The truth is that he came there having heard that we were selling some of the treasures from the estate. The money which we'd brought with us was disappearing rapidly, and I saw no recourse but to sell some things to get money for us to continue living there.

The merchant bought three of the items, and paid a decent price for them, though I knew well he'd sell them for far more. He wanted a fourth, but offered much less than I felt the piece was worth. We haggled for a time, and then he made his offer. He had three daughters, and would allow one of them to come to serve me for a year, if I'd agree to his price.

I thought about it for a while. It would be nice to have someone to take over some of the household chores, leaving me free to do more studying. And His Highness would be grateful to have a wench again. At last I agreed, with the reservation that he had to bring her to me for my approval before taking the vase.

He brought Anna the next day, a comely fifteen-year-old with a ready smile and reasonably decent manners. I accepted her, with the provision that if she left before the year was up, he would pay me fifty gold pieces to make up for it. He beamed happily and took the vase with hardly a backward look at her. So much for her being his favorite and beloved daughter.

I showed the girl the kitchen and her room, then explained that we kept wild animals in the garden and she must never go out there, under any circumstances.

Things went along well for a week or two. I enspelled her to make sure her courses stayed regular, and then gave her to my master for a sleeping companion. This meant I had less opportunity for pleasing him now, but he was happier, and that's all that mattered.

She'd been there for a month when she saw him change. She was standing in the garden door looking out when the beast staggered near her and collapsed, slowly becoming my master. When I got there, she was standing wide-eyed, her hands over her mouth to hold back her screams. I harshly ordered her to her room, then helped him to the baths.

When he was in bed, I went to her room. She was lying across the bed, weeping.

"So now you know the truth," I said.

"I've been sleeping with that monster," she sobbed.

"No. The beast is the result of a foul spell. His Highness is fated to suffer that during the day, and only at night may he be his own true self. You've given some solace to him. Are you to withdraw it now?"

She sat up, drying her eyes. "Do you swear it?"

"Yes."

"No one must ever know that I've done this," she said firmly.

"No one will ever know unless you tell it yourself."

"All right," she said. "I'll go to him then. But you must pay me for it."

They say she slowly fell in love with him during the months she was with us. In truth she bedded with him and kept house for us, and just bided her time waiting for her year to be up. And when it was up, she left without even saying goodbye to him.

That night, I gave him a long slow massage.

"Where's Anna?" he asked.

My hands stilled for a moment, then continued their movements.

"Her father sold her to us for one year, and the year was up today. She's gone," I told him quietly.

He was silent for a few moments, then buried his face in the pillow. "I see," he said, voice muffled.

I massaged his buttocks particularly well, letting my finger slide down into the crack to stroke his anus. And at last I told him to turn over.

He did so. The pillow was wet, but his tears had stopped. I massaged his front slowly and thoroughly, then lowered my mouth to his balls, sucking them gently. Then I moved to his cock and sucked it as I'd learned he liked best. Slow and easy at first, then getting more passionate as his pelvis began moving rhythmically under me. I'd learned how to prevent gagging finally, and could take him all the way to the root, and now I did so, sucking feverishly, wanting all of him that I could have for the time that he could be mine.

He fell asleep at once, his body drained. I watched him sleeping for a while, the longing in me bringing tears to my eyes. I knelt by the bed then and kissed his hand, wishing I could take his place. What would it matter if I were the beast?

I wept then, more than I ever had, silently so as not to wake him. When the tears stopped at last, I kissed him gently and went back to my studies.

It was scarcely two hours before dawn when he woke and came out to the study.

"Have you made any progress at all?" he asked.

"Perhaps," I said. "This new manuscript has information about similar spells. It says that they feed on the hate and anger and bitterness inside the person enspelled. That the only way to overcome them is with love, which will overcome those emotions."

"Love?" he said sarcastically. "And how am I to find love when I'm a beast all day long?"

He wheeled sharply and left the room. I bowed my head and wept again. The love was there waiting for him, if he could only see past the veil of servitude through which he saw me.

The next day, I went back to the merchant and contracted for another year of Anna's service. The price was another of the magnificent vases, but I thought it would be worth it if she could grow to love him.

He seemed a bit happier, at first. But then he asked why she'd returned. I told him the truth, and he went silent again, as he did sometimes.

She stayed for a month, then refused to stay any longer. He wasn't nice to her anymore, she said, and she wouldn't tolerate it. She packed her things and left. I sat in the study the rest of the afternoon, unable to concentrate, wondering how he was going to react to the news that she was gone.

I gave him another massage that night, to try to make up for it. When he turned over onto his back, his cock was throbbing and red. I could hardly complete the massage for wanting it. When I moved to it at last, I looked up at him. Always, his eyes were closed when I touched him. But this time they were open. He was watching me. I swallowed hard, not sure of what to do. Then slowly, I lowered my mouth to his balls and sucked them gently. He closed his eyes for a moment, then opened them and continued watching me. I couldn't bear it. I closed my eyes as I lowered my mouth to his cock, sucking it gently, as he liked, then slowly increasing the pace, allowing myself to suck it as greedily as I wanted to. When he exploded into my mouth, I swallowed it all hungrily, licking the last residue from his cock, and then my eyes opened.

He was still staring at me, and when my eyes met his, something happened to me. I began very slowly moving up to his face, like a fish being pulled in on a line. When my head was directly above his, I started to lower my mouth to his.

And he closed his eyes and turned his head away.

It was like plunging naked into a chilly river. I drew away from him, my back to him to hide the sudden tears which poured from my eyes. He was silent, and I stayed silent as well.

When I regained control of myself, I surreptitiously wiped my eyes, and then turned to help him to the bed. He was already there, asleep.

I stumbled into the study and dropped my head onto my arms, sobbing helplessly. How could I have been such an utter fool, to think that a prince would want to be kissed by someone like me? It would be like kissing his dog or his horse!

I don't know how long I cried there that night, but at last the hurt was washed away, replaced by a dull ache deep down inside. I looked at the manuscript, and then suddenly hurled it from me. Who was I to think I could learn enough sorcery to counter the spell of such a strong sorcerer? I was just a servant, not a sorcerer. I got up and went to my pallet across his door, and fell into a deep sleep, in which dreams of him kissing me alternated with dreams of him shoving me away.

It was after dawn when I awoke, and he was already gone. I made breakfast and did the morning chores, then dealt with the merchant when he came to call. He insisted that he owed me nothing since the girl had been mistreated. When I denied that she'd been mistreated, he made her bare her back and show me the wicked scratches on it. I sighed then, and gave in. It didn't seem to matter anymore.

That evening, I helped my master to the baths, but I made no move to pleasure him, even when his cock bobbed hard and red as I washed it. I bathed him carefully, helped him to the bed, and wished him a good night. Then I curled up on my pallet and tried to sleep.

When sleep refused to come, thanks to my own throbbing cock, I went out to the gardens, thinking a walk would help to relax me. I walked through the flowers close to the house, coming to a small fountain with a stone bench around it. I sat down, wondering what was to become of both of us. Would he kill himself at last in one of his crazed fits? Or would he come into the house and kill me? Would the girl tell what she'd seen, and bring the authorities down on us? Would things go on as they were, and if so, how would I get the money for supplies? There was a limit to how much could be sold from the estate. Perhaps I could get a job in the city. But doing what? I had no skills worth selling.

I sighed and buried my face in my hands, with helpless sobs of pain and fear. I'd been charged with taking care of him, and I'd failed. His father was probably dead now anyway. His whole family was gone, most likely. No one would know I'd failed him so. Only me.

I don't know how long I sat there, long enough that the night chill soaked into my very bones. I was shivering when I sought my pallet at last, still with no answers to any of my questions.

The next morning, I woke with a fever, and cursed myself for the too-long excursion in the night. I staggered into the kitchen and made a brew of herbs and honey to fight the fever.

All day long I chilled, unable to get warm in spite of fires built high and hot drinks one after the other. When darkness fell, I staggered to the garden and was unable to lift him, and him in too much of a stupor to help himself, as he often was. I pulled him onto a rug and dragged it through the house to the baths, rolled him into the hot water, and then stripped and followed him in. I passed out for a few minutes, and when I came to, he was staring at me.

"What's wrong?" he asked.

"Chills and fever," I whispered. "I'll be all right soon."

He shook his head and lay back in the water. "We're a fine pair, aren't we?" he said, his voice weary and sad.

"Yes, Highness," I whispered, unable to fight the hot tears which filled my eyes.

He sat up and washed the filth from himself. Then he began bathing me, though I protested. When he finished, he dried both of us off, and then we helped each other over to the bed.

"Get in there and cover up good," he ordered.

"Highness, I can't take your bed!" I cried. "Where would you sleep?"

"Right here next to you. The warmth of my body will chase the chills away. Lie down. That's an order."

I obeyed, and he stretched out next to me, holding me close, all the covers pulled up over us. I went to sleep almost at once, but it was a feverish sleep, with dreams coming and going, dreams of him holding me and loving me as much as I loved him. And nightmares of him turning away from me, making me sob helplessly.

When I woke, it was past dawn and he was gone. On the table next to the bed was a pot of herbal tea, with a candle to keep it warm for me. Tears filled my eyes as I poured it into a cup and drank.

I got up at noon and staggered into the kitchen to make more of the tea. The fire was out, and I had to struggle to rebuild it. I had finally succeeded, and put water on to boil, when I felt eyes on me. I looked up, and the beast was standing in the doorway, staring at me.

Every muscle in my body went limp. I knew I couldn't escape from him even if I was well, and I certainly couldn't do it now, in this condition. I closed my eyes and bowed my head, accepting the inevitable.

When several minutes went by without a sound, I looked up. He was gone. I stared at the empty doorway in shock, wondering if I'd dreamed it.

I drank more of the tea, and sat before the fire, trying to recover my strength as rapidly as I could. But when darkness came, I was no better. I staggered out to the garden. He was just changing, and I turned away, unable to bear watching.

When I turned back to him, he was on his hands and knees, trying to stand. I staggered over to him.

"Lie down on the rug, Highness, and I'll drag you to the bath," I said, my voice hoarse beyond belief.

He shook his head, and managed to get to his feet, swaying a little. I put my arm around his waist, and he put his around my shoulders, and together we staggered to the bath.

After the bath, he was a little stronger, and helped me over to the bed. Then he disappeared, and came back with a pot of the herbal tea. I wept again.

"Highness, it isn't your job to wait on me," I tried to protest.

"Shut up," he said quietly. "Who'll take care of me if I let you die of this? Drink it, then lie down and let me get you warm."

I obeyed, and again I slept in his arms, the torture of it almost more than I could bear.

Again when I awoke, he was gone, and the tea was on the table for me, with some bread. I hadn't eaten anything the day before, but the bread reminded me that I must, to keep my strength up as much as possible. I forced it down and drank the tea, then fell asleep again.

This went on for five days and nights, until the fever broke and left me. I felt unbearably weakened, but whole once more, and began eating again to try to regain my strength. That night, he started to help me to his bed, and I told him, almost reluctantly, that the fever was gone. He hesitated for a moment, then continued on his way.

"Nonetheless, you don't have your strength back yet. You'll sleep here until you're completely well again."

Three nights later, when I was well again, I decided to have one more night of the closeness of him, and I let him take me to the bed. He snuggled me close, my back against his chest, and his hard cock pressing against my bottom, making gooseflesh ripple across my buttocks. One of his arms was under me, and the other around my waist. As my cock swelled in response to him, I felt the tip of it touch his arm. I didn't know what to do. If I tried to move away from his arm, it would send my buttocks back harder against his cock. And if I didn't, he'd know I was hard from being so close to him.

Then his arm moved, and his hand slipped down to encircle my cock. My breath stopped for a moment. He'd never touched me before.

His breath was warm against my neck as he whispered, "May I take you?"

I nodded, unable to speak.

He took his hand from my cock and lifted my leg, spreading my buttocks, and positioning his cock against my

85

anus, which was pulsating wildly. He smeared the fluid from the tip of his cock over the head, and then slipped it inside me. It hurt, but I gritted my teeth and tried not to tighten up on him. He withdrew a little and then moved a little farther in, continuing until he was completely embedded in me. When he was fully inside, he stopped moving, giving my body time to adjust to him. I sighed, feeling almost dizzy from the pleasure which was replacing the pain.

It was my beloved master whose cock was splitting me. If only he'd touch me again. But even as I thought it, his arm came around me and his hand encircled my cock. A low moan escaped from my lips, and he started moving then, slowly and easily. By the time he started moving rapidly, the rapture had overtaken me, and I was soaring high above the room. When he drove into me and I felt his cock pulsating, his hand tightened on me, and I came, harder than I'd ever come in my life.

His arms tightened for a moment, then relaxed, and he whispered, "Good night."

Incredible peace washed through me. "Good night, my beloved prince," I whispered.

I realized what I'd said just before sleep claimed me, but it was too late to call back the secret name I'd never said aloud before.

When I woke, less than an hour before dawn, he was asleep, but hard again with a morning erection. It had almost slipped from me, but I moved down on it, capturing it fully, and slowly began moving on it, my hips pumping up and down. He came awake then, with a low chuckle, and

WANDA WOLFE   *Beauty and the Beast*

his hand came around me to capture my cock and take me with him to bliss. When we came, he held me for a few moments, then slipped out of me and quietly left. I lay there in the bed, unable to believe what had happened the night before.

Maybe he didn't love me as I did him, but this was as close as I was going to get to that love. And as long as he wanted me, I was going to be available for him.

For a while, this renewed my energy and my interest in trying to find an answer to the puzzle. I didn't work at night anymore, though, preferring to sleep in his arms for as long as he allowed me to remain in his bed. He always took me like that, with us lying on our sides, my back to his chest. And he was always kind enough to stroke my cock and give me release, too. Though I'm not so sure I couldn't have come just from having his cock in me.

Two weeks went by like this, and then one morning, I woke near dawn, to find him hard inside me, his cock moving slowly. I snuggled back against him, welcoming him, and his arm came around me to encircle my cock.

"Do you think the change would take me if we were still doing this at dawn?" he asked thoughtfully.

My blood chilled. "I don't know," I whispered.

He held me closer. "But what do you think would happen?" he insisted.

I closed my eyes, knowing that tone of voice. "I'm willing to try if you want to, Highness," I whispered.

"This is such a peaceful thing. I don't see how the change could come upon me during this."

I surreptitiously wiped away the tears that filled my eyes. "Neither do I, Highness. Certainly it will work."

He slowed his movements. "Then we must make it last," he murmured.

I closed my eyes. "Highness, may I beg a favor of you?" I asked.

"All right. What is it?"

My voice came out husky. "I've been in love with you for years. And I've longed for you to kiss me. When the moment comes, will you kiss me, please?"

"Can you turn over enough for that?" he asked, after a long hesitation.

I shifted my shoulders enough to bring the back of my head onto the pillow.

"Can you do it like this?" I asked.

He lifted himself a little and checked, his lips very lightly touching mine. "Yes."

I closed my eyes, my heart pounding. Who'd take care of him with me gone? Who would arrange for the sheep he needed, and all the other little details of life? But that would have to be his problem now. He was willing to trade my service to him for a crazy experiment which would cost my life. In spite of the love he'd shown me lately, I was still no more to him than his horse or his dog. The ache in my chest was so strong I didn't really mind dying, just to get rid of the hurt.

The window lightened, and I felt the first hint of the change in his skin. He felt it, too, and lowered his mouth to mine. His kiss was skilled and deep, making me dizzy.

Oh, by all the gods, if I had to die, let it be like this!

My anus began stretching then, as the beast cock began expanding. My breath quickened as the pain built. Soon it would stretch to its limit, and then it would tear, my blood spilling down over those giant beast balls. A sob caught deep in my throat and I threw my arm around him, feeling not my beloved master, but the fur of the beast.

The pain overwhelmed me then, and merciful darkness carried me down.

I woke there in his bed, weak and dizzy. The sheets were stiff under me, and I knew it was my blood which had made them so. I hadn't died then, but I'd lost a lot of blood, or I wouldn't be so faint. I tried to sit up, but the room swirled around and blackness threatened again.

By the sun through the window, I knew it was near noon. I had to have something to drink to replace all the blood I'd lost. I tried again to sit up, but couldn't. I slumped back against the pillows.

Then the door opened. I stared, not believing it. My master was coming toward me, with a tray containing food and drink. He smiled at the look on my face.

"You look like you're seeing a ghost," he said cheerfully.

"It's daylight out. You're not—" I stopped.

He sat down on the side of the bed, and lifted my head, holding a cup to my lips. I drank thirstily. It was the herbal tea, thick with honey.

"No, I'm not," he said when he took the empty cup away. "Thanks to you."

"Me?" I whispered.

"Yes, you," he said tenderly. "You loved me enough to risk your very life for me. And when I felt that love washing through me as I kissed you, the hatred and bitterness all washed away, and the beast started losing his hold on me. He wasn't able to take me. And I don't think he ever will again."

"Thank the gods," I sobbed. "Highness, I'm so happy you'll never have to go through that again."

He wiped the tears away. "Why did you never tell me before how you felt about me?" he asked, his voice gentle.

My face burned. "I had no right. I'm but your servant, and you're my prince."

"I know. Your beloved prince," he said softly. So he had heard that. He took my hand in his. "But this morning, you told me. Why?"

"I thought I was going to die. I couldn't die without a kiss from you, and I knew you'd never do it unless I told you the truth."

"Why did you think I wouldn't do it without that?"

I turned my face away. "Why would you ever want to kiss me?"

"I've wanted to kiss you many times, and I never let myself do it."

"Why?" I gasped.

"Because I was afraid," he admitted.

"Afraid of what?"

"The depth of my feelings for you. And fear that you didn't return those feelings."

My head whirled, and I fell back against the pillow.

"Don't die on me now," he whispered. And lifted my head to drink more of the tea.

"I think I must be dreaming," I said, tears racing down my face.

"Don't cry. You've lost too much fluid already. Just drink this and then sleep some more. We'll talk later."

I obeyed him, too weak to do anything else.

Every time I woke during the next two days, he was there to take care of me. And finally the time came when I was able to make it over to the bath with his help. I settled back into the hot water with a sigh of relief. He left me there to go change the sheets on the bed, then when he'd finished with that, he joined me in the water.

"I did remember a little of my sorcery," he said quietly. "Enough to stop the bleeding and heal the tears in your body. But even so, I think I ought to wait a few days before trying to take you, if you'll ever trust me to do that again."

His hand was very close to mine, and I took it, lifting it to my lips to kiss. "I trust you completely, Highness. In all things."

He shook his head. "You shouldn't. You warned me that damned sorcerer wasn't to be trusted, and I ignored you. Don't let me do that again. None of this would have happened if I'd only listened to you in the first place." He took a deep breath. "You told me that you loved me. Did you mean it?"

I bowed my head. "Yes, my prince."

"How long have you felt that way?"

"Since we were eleven."

"I wish you had told me a long time ago."

"I had no right to tell you anything like that. I'm but your servant, Highness."

"You're more than my servant, and you know it. You're brother, confidant, friend, companion, lover. And for the past two years, you were mother and caretaker to me as well. I don't know if I'll be able to reclaim our kingdom or not, but if I do, I swear to you that I'll give you the highest title in the land, and treat you always as my first adviser."

I hesitantly moved a little closer to him, and he put an arm around my waist and drew me close to him. "Do you—" I began, but stopped, unable to ask the question which tormented me.

He tilted my face up and kissed away the tears, then kissed my lips gently. "Do I love you?" he asked softly. "Is that what you want to ask and are afraid to hear the answer to?"

I swallowed, eyes closed, then nodded.

"Look at me," he commanded.

My eyes flew open and I looked up at him. He grinned.

"Old habits are hard to break, aren't they?" he teased. "The answer is yes. I do love you."

I felt as though my heart would burst from my chest. I laid my head on his shoulder, and he held me close to him, his arms warm around my body. He loved me. Oh, by all the gods, he loved me!

And you boys know the rest of the story. We sold the estate, and returned here to do battle with the foul sorcerer who'd taken over the kingdom. Between the two of us, working together, we were able to overcome him, and restore the kingdom to its rightful rulers again. His Majesty was in a dungeon, his health nearly broken. But he recovered enough to rule another ten years. Then His Highness took the throne and ruled for another forty, before abdicating in favor of his son, your father, who rules today.

And here he comes now, still handsome even in his old age. Sit here beside me, old friend, and help me amuse these boys. They've been having me tell them the tale of Beauty and the Beast, though I told them that indeed Beauty was no beauty, and won not your heart.

You boys, stop laughing and pay him no mind. I'm no beauty now and I was no beauty then! 'Tis only in his own eyes that I look good.

Here comes your tutor and you must go to your lessons now. Learn them well, lest another foul sorcerer come to take what is rightfully yours.

Look at them run, my beloved prince. They do remind me so of us when we were that age. I wish we still had some of that boundless energy.

Why, yes, my heart, I do believe I could get up enough energy for that, if we do it slow and easy. Let's go to my room. No one will disturb us there.

About the Contributors

GARY BOWEN is the author of the novel *Diary of a Vampire* (Masquerade Books, 1995) and his short fiction has appeared in magazines and anthologies far too numerous to list. A collection of his erotic science fiction short stories, *Queer Destinies*, was published by Circlet Press in 1994, and a collection of erotic fiction, *Man Hungry*, is forthcoming from BadBoy Books in 1996. Obelesk Books published *Winter of the Soul*, a collection of his gay vampire fiction, in 1995. His next project is editing a collection of erotic gay western fiction for Masquerade Books.

EVAN HOLLANDER writes fantasy, science fiction, and erotic stories and is best known for combining all three in men's publications such as *Gent*. *Virtual Girls*, a collection of his best erotic science fiction was recently published by Circlet Press. He also has stories in the Circlet anthologies *Technosex* and *Selling Venus*.

LISA HUNT, the cover artist, is a professional illustrator whose published work has included commissions for Simon & Schuster, Llewellyn, *Marion Zimmer Bradley's Fantasy Magazine, Asimov's*, and *Analog*. Lisa is a member of the Association of Science Fiction and Fantasy Artists and is currently at work producing paintings for a tarot deck. She lives with her husband and four cats in south Florida.

DAVID LAURENTS is the editor of *The BadBoy Book of Erotic Poetry* and *Wanderlust: Homoerotic Tales of Travel* (both from Masquerade Books, 1995), among other books. His work appears in *Wired Hard*

(Circlet Press, 1994) and many other erotic anthologies and magazines.

E R STEWART is a prolific mind whose creative works include fiction, nonfiction, criticism, maps, cartoons, poetry, and more ... which can be found in *Year's Best Fantasy and Horror, Analog, Aboriginal SF, Marion Zimmer Bradley's Fantasy Magazine,* Baen's *WarWorld* series, just to mention a few of the sf/f outlets.

WANDA WOLFE has been writing nonfiction for many years and has had many articles published in the *Mensa Bulletin* and other publications. "The Frog Prince" and "Beauty and the Beast" are her first published works of fiction. She is currently the editor of *LeGambit,* the newsletter of the gay and lesbian special-interest group of Mensa.